**MICHAELE RAZI**

# FRANK the Seven-Legged Spider

little bigfoot

an imprint of sasquatch books
seattle, wa

Frank likes being a spider.

He likes making beautiful webs.

He likes scaring silly humans.

But most of all, he really likes having
eight legs—eight beautiful, glorious legs.

Legs that can wiggle

 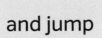 

and jump

and scurry around.

Everything was going great until . . .

he woke up missing a leg.

Is he still a spider? Frank doesn't know.
Well, that settles it. He has to find his leg.

Of course, moving around with a missing
leg takes a bit of practice.

But Frank gets the hang of it and he
goes out to search for his leg.

Oh! Is Frank's leg here,
up in this strange tree?

*No, that's not my leg.*

Is it here, underneath this squishy rock?

No, that's not my leg.

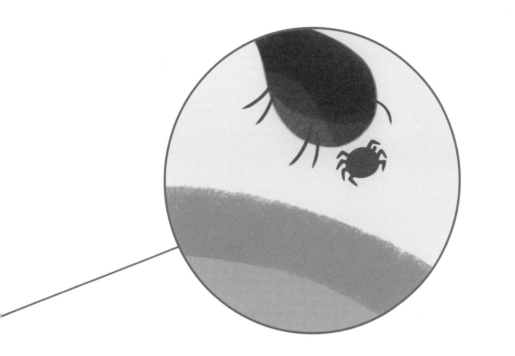

Is it here, in this dark, warm cave?

*No, that's not my leg!*

Frank searches everywhere
and still can't find his leg!

What is he now?

He doesn't know.

And I can still wiggle my legs

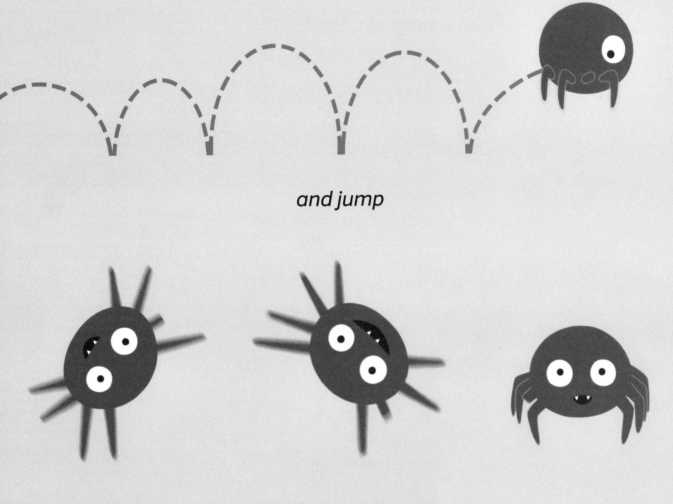

and jump

and scurry around.

That must mean I'm still a . . .

To Mick, there are not enough
thank-yous in the world

———————————

Manufactured in China by C&C Offset Printing Co. Ltd.
Shenzhen, Guangdong Province, in May 2017

Published by Little Bigfoot, an imprint of Sasquatch Books

21 20 19 18 17      9 8 7 6 5 4 3 2 1

Editors: Ben Clanton, Christy Cox
Production editor: Emma Reh
Design: Anna Goldstein

Library of Congress Cataloging-in-Publication Data is available.

ISBN: 978-1-63217-128-3

Sasquatch Books
1904 3rd Avenue, Suite 710 | Seattle, WA 98101
(206) 467-4300 | custserv@sasquatchbooks.com
www.sasquatchbooks.com